# The Elves and the Shoemakers

A Tale by the Brothers Grimm

Retold by Jeanne Willis
Illustrated by Claire Tindall

Mollie and Ollie made very good shoes.
They lived and worked together.
To make good shoes they had to use the very softest leather.

The cost of leather went up and up.
They had no money for more.
The very last pair of shoes was sold.
Now Mollie and Ollie were poor.

A bit of red leather was all they had.
They shut the shop and went to bed.

"No money for leather, no leather for shoes. We've nothing to sell," they said.

In the night, six elves came in.
They sat down in a row.
They snipped the leather and stitched some shoes, the finest they could sew.

"Did you make these shoes, dear Mollie? They're lovely!" Ollie said.

A rich man came and bought the shoes.
"You make good shoes," he said.
"Here is the money to make some more.
Make me a hundred pairs in red."

"They must be made by Friday noon
for that's my wedding day,
and if those pairs of shoes are late,
I shall refuse to pay."

Ollie said yes, they would make them!
But Mollie said, "What shall we do?
We'll never make a hundred pairs
in time, just me and you."

"Mollie, I wonder who made those shoes," said Ollie, "Let's hide tonight and see. Whoever made those might make some more. How splendid that would be."

Late that night they hid themselves.
They peeped from behind the door.
They saw six snipping, clipping elves,
all sitting on the shoe shop floor.

They sang this song, "New shoes to stitch, a hundred pairs will make them rich. Let's all snip and clip and stitch them well. Mollie and Ollie need shoes to sell."

For seven nights they stitched and snipped.
The shoes were heeled and soled.
But as they stitched, they shivered,
for the shoe shop floor was cold.

So Mollie made them little coats
to stop the elves from freezing,
and little caps and matching scarves,
in case they started sneezing.

The elves got dressed and cried with joy, "We're warm, all thanks to you!"

Mollie and Ollie sold all the shoes. Now they are rich and happy too.